THIS WALKER BOOK BELONGS TO:

_____

_____

_____

_____

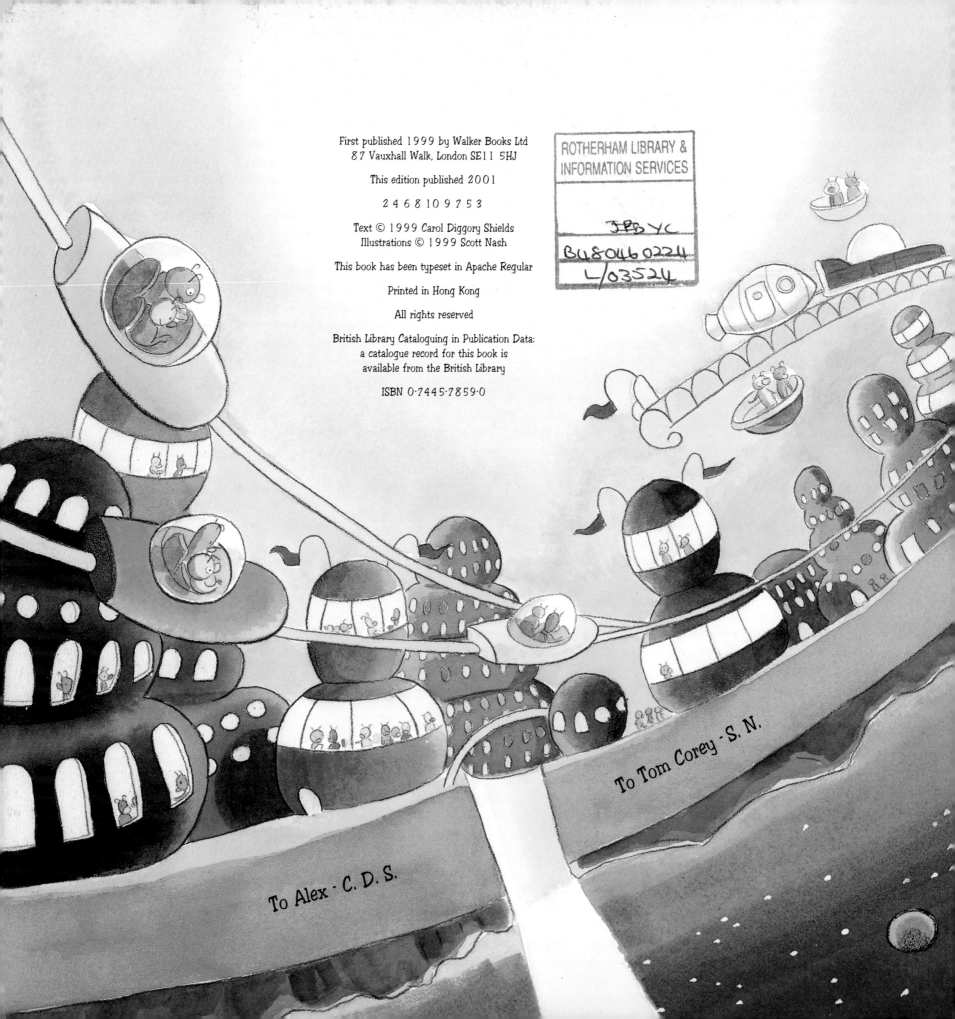

First published 1999 by Walker Books Ltd
87 Vauxhall Walk, London SE11 5HJ

This edition published 2001

2 4 6 8 10 9 7 5 3

Text © 1999 Carol Diggory Shields
Illustrations © 1999 Scott Nash

This book has been typeset in Apache Regular

Printed in Hong Kong

British Library Cataloguing in Publication Data:
a catalogue record for this book is
available from the British Library

ISBN 0·7445·7859·0

To Alex · C. D. S.

To Tom Corey · S. N.

MARTIAN ROCK

written by
Carol Diggory Shields

illustrated by
Scott Nash

WALKER BOOKS
AND SUBSIDIARIES
LONDON · BOSTON · SYDNEY

"Attention all life forms,
simple and complex!
Tune in your antennae
and flex your necks –
Our brave explorers of the solar system
Blast off in ten quadsecs,
and how we will miss them!"

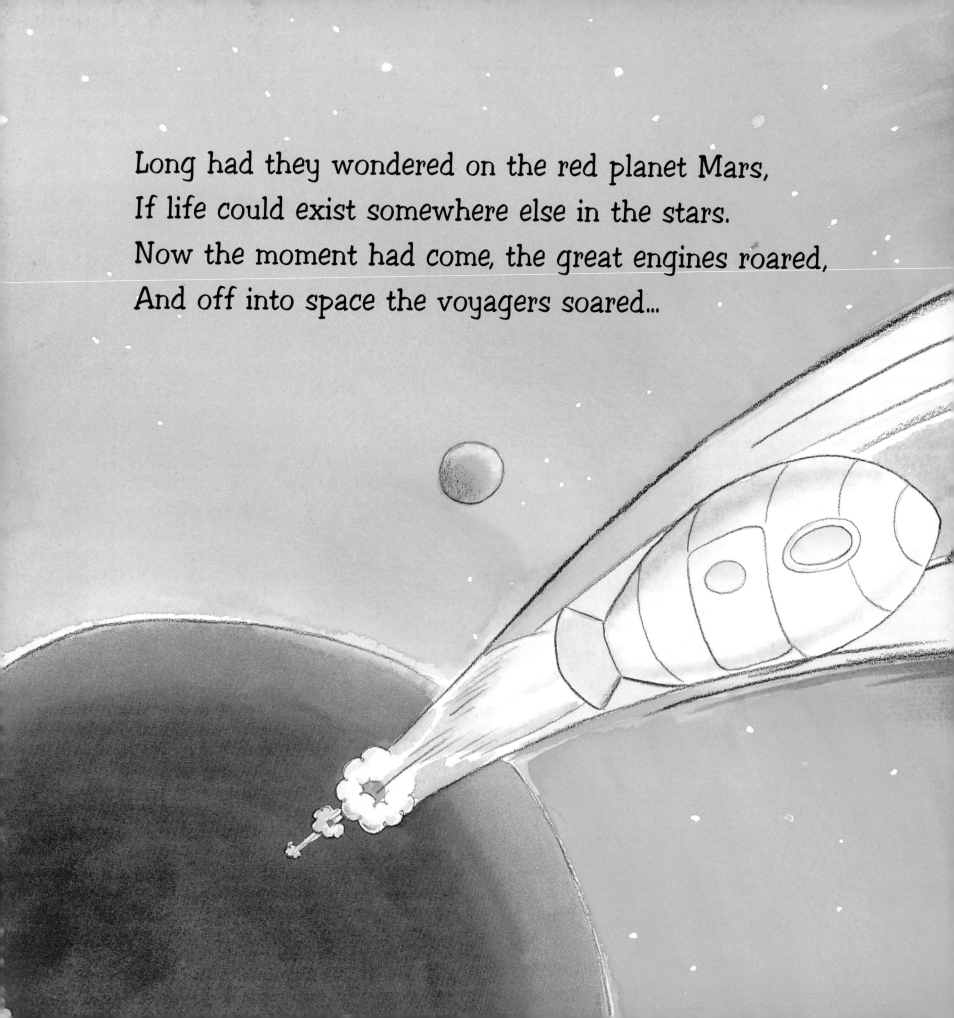

Long had they wondered on the red planet Mars,
If life could exist somewhere else in the stars.
Now the moment had come, the great engines roared,
And off into space the voyagers soared...

Their first destination
was Orb Number Nine,
The outermost planet,
so the trip took some time.

It was dreary and dark,
   and mostly all granite.
They radioed home –
   "No life on this planet."

They flew on to Eight,
   the one that's deep blue,
And counted eight moons
   (Mars only has two).
Winds howled and whistled
   in storms of blue snow.
Not a life form in sight
   at two hundred below.

More moons circled Seven
(they counted fifteen),
And it rolled on its side
and glowed sickly green.
It was slushy and smelly,
with no living things.
So they went on to Six,
with the bright yellow rings.

Those rings were just junk,
and the planet all gas.
There was no place to land,
so they flew straight on past.

Orb Five was red-orange,
    magnetic, immense,
And covered with clouds
    that were swirling and dense.

Amid thunder and lightning,
    they decided to beat it:
"If anything lives here
    we don't want to meet it!"

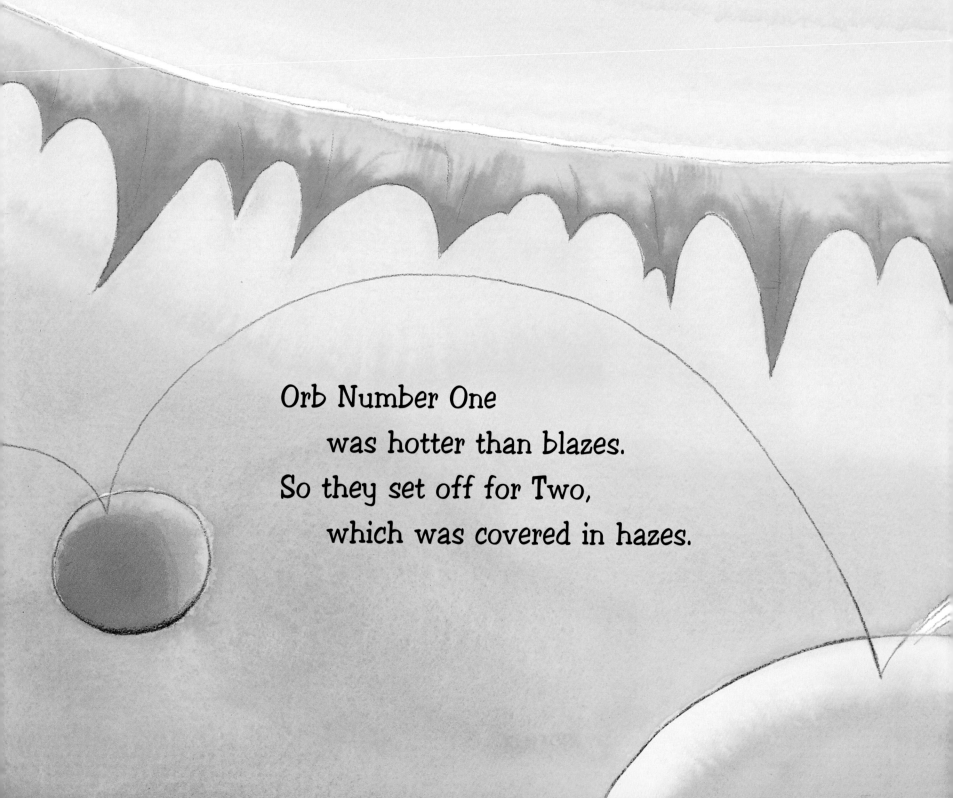

They rode faster and faster, into the Sun,
And didn't slow down till Orb Number One.

Orb Number One
    was hotter than blazes.
So they set off for Two,
    which was covered in hazes.

But Orb Two was worse
with acid rain pelting...

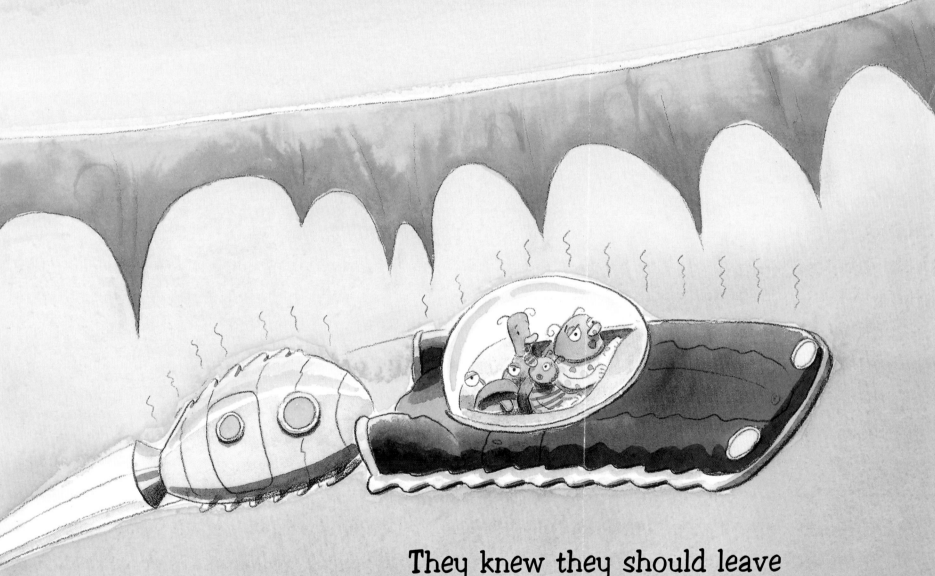

They knew they should leave
when the ship started melting!

By now they were homesick,
filled with despair,
And clean out of socks
and fresh underwear.

"There's nobody out here.
We're all alone.
We'll glance at Orb Three,
then let's head for home."

They buzzed the South Pole, saw nothing but snow.
"It's cold and it's empty," they sighed. "Let's just go."

But as the crew flagged, the Captain declared,
"Hey! Wait a quadsec –
there's something out there!"

They looked out of the ship
  and saw he was right –
An alien life form
  strolled slowly in sight!
It came close, very close,
  with a waddling walk,
And greeted the crew
  with a nod and a squawk.

Then from the horizon more came by the dozen:
Grandparents, babies, aunts, uncles and cousins!
They surrounded the craft in a jostling pack.
The Martians were scared. Were they under attack?

But the life forms were friendly and quite unafraid.
The Martians soon joined in the games that they played,

Like Follow-the-Leader

and Slippery-Sliding,

Tummy-Toboggan

and Find-Me-I'm-Hiding.

They showed off their diving, invited them in.
(The Martians said no, because Martians can't swim.)

The Martians phoned home.
"We need wonder no more —
Life has been found
on the planet
next door!"

Their mission accomplished, the crew had to go.
"We'll miss you," they said to their friends in the snow.
"But keep on evolving - some day you might fly!
Then you visit us - our orb is close by."

And they left their new friends
with a fine souvenir:
A lasting reminder that
The Martians were here!

Martian name: **MARTIAN ROCK**
("a fine souvenir")
Earth name: **ALH 84001**

ALH 84001, a fifteen-centimetre-
long meteorite believed to be
from Mars, was found on
Antarctica in 1984. Antarctica
is one of the best places on
Earth to find meteorites
because they're so easy to
spot on Antarctica's many ice-
fields. Thousands of meteorites have been
discovered there, some of which are
thought to be from Mars. But ALH 84001
is unlike any other Martian meteorite.
Scientists discovered microscopic features
in it that resemble ancient bacteria on
Earth. This discovery sparked a debate
about whether or not they might be
fossils of ancient Martian life – a debate
that is still going on today!

Pluto is the furthest planet from the Sun –
mostly. But its orbit does, at times, bring Pluto
closer to the Sun than the next nearest planet,
Neptune. Pluto is a bluish colour and has one
very large moon, Charon. Pluto's surface is
very dark in places, but brighter in areas
covered by solid ices of nitrogen, methane
and carbon monoxide. The temperature is,
on average, a very chilly -230ºC!

Martian name: **ORB 8**
Earth name: **NEPTUNE**

Martian name: **ORB 9**
Earth name: **PLUTO**

Neptune has stronger winds
than any of the other planets.
Giant hurricanes circle the planet,
and one of them is as wide as the
Earth! And because Neptune is so far from the Sun,
the average temperature is about -220ºC. The planet
has eight moons and gets its deep blue colour from
methane gas in its very cloudy atmosphere.

Uranus is the only planet
that doesn't rotate on its
north and south poles,
but tilted on its side. The
planet has ten rings and
fifteen moons. Uranus is
believed to have a small
rocky core surrounded
by an unpleasant
combination of
water, ammonia
and methane
gases and ices.

Martian name: **ORB 7**
Earth name: **URANUS**

Martian name: **ORB 6**
Earth name: **SATURN**

Saturn has
numerous rings
that are believed to
be made up of chunks
of ice and snow, and possibly pieces of moons
that were smashed by comets and other objects.
Saturn is mostly made up of hydrogen, with
smaller amounts of helium and methane. It has
eighteen known moons – and the Hubble space
telescope recently spotted four new objects
orbiting the planet that might be moons as well!

Martian name: **ORB 5**
Earth name: **JUPITER**

Jupiter is the largest planet in the solar system. The planet has a strong magnetic field that stretches millions of kilometres into space, and a powerful ever-changing system of clouds and storms. One of these storms, the Great Red Spot, is over three hundred years old and, in places, is twice as wide as Earth. Jupiter has twelve moons, and scientists believe one of them, Europa, might have a water ocean lurking beneath its icy surface – the possibility of life existing here is under investigation!

Towards the end of the eighteenth century, scientists predicted that there should be another planet between the orbits of Jupiter and Mars. In time, it was discovered that there are actually many smaller objects, asteroids, orbiting the Sun in this region. Some of these asteroids might have been captured by the pull of Mars and Jupiter, becoming moons of the two planets.

Martian name: **THE ASTEROID BELT**
Earth name: **THE ASTEROID BELT**

Martian name: **ORB 3**
Earth name: **EARTH**

Like Mars, Earth has a very varied landscape. Unlike Mars, Earth's atmosphere is made up mostly of nitrogen, with smaller amounts of oxygen, and it has water oceans. Earth is teeming with life forms "simple and complex" – from redwood trees to raccoons, penguins to plankton, hippopotamuses to humans.

Martian name: **MARS**
Earth name: **MARS**

Mars is a planet of low-lying plains, giant volcanic mountains, massive canyons, sweeping dunes of red sand and craters of all sizes. The average temperature is about -63ºC and huge wind-storms often rage over large portions of the planet. Mars has two very small moons, Deimos and Phobos, that orbit very near the planet.

Martian name: **ORB 2**
Earth name: **VENUS**

Venus is covered in thick, swirling cloud. From far away, it looks as if it could be Earth's sister planet. But the two planets are very different. Venus is surrounded by a dense atmosphere of carbon dioxide that traps sunlight and creates a terrible greenhouse effect. As a result, the average surface temperature is a scorching 482ºC – even hotter than the temperature on Mercury!

Martian name: **ORB 1**
Earth name: **MERCURY**

Mercury is the closest planet to the Sun. It has almost no atmosphere, so its sky is always black. Mercury is very hot – around 174ºC. Its surface looks very like that of Earth's moon, with dusty hills and ancient craters of all sizes marking the surface.

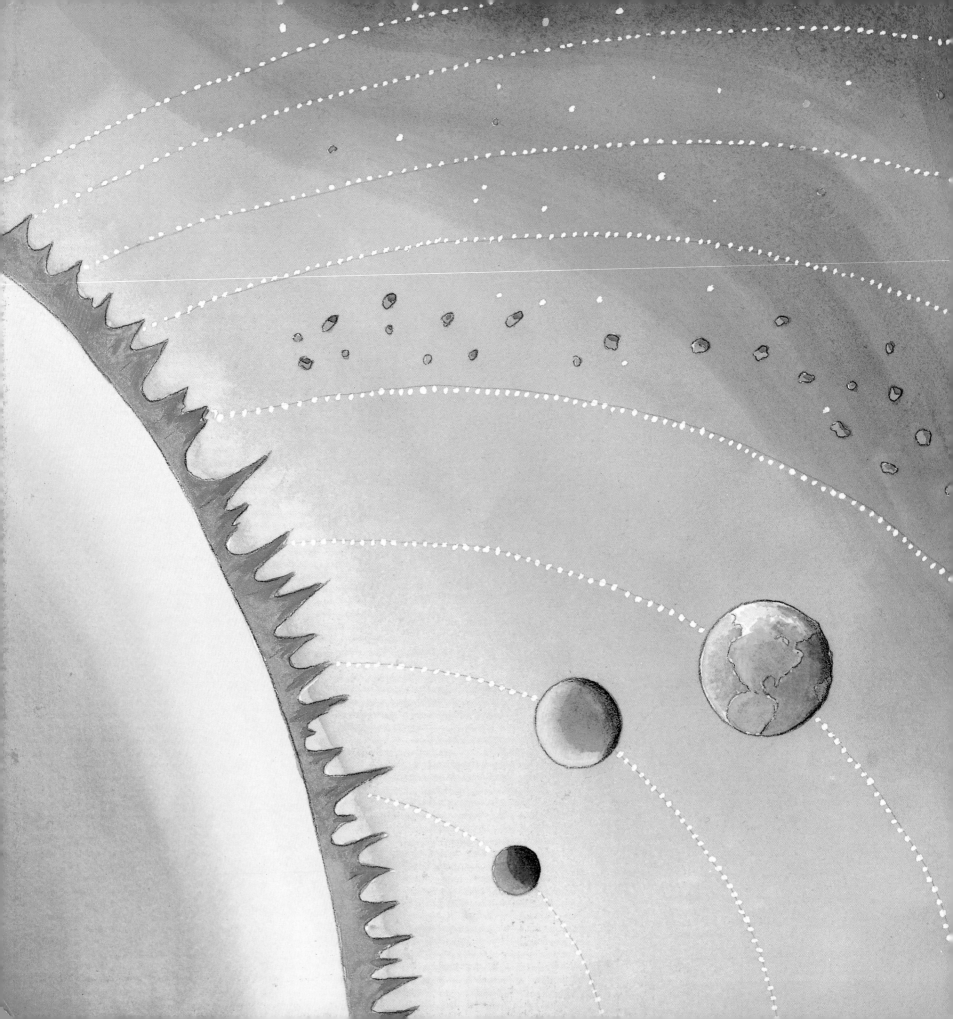

CAROL DIGGORY SHIELDS credits Scott Nash with the original idea for **Martian Rock**. She says, "Scott was curious about the origin of a meteorite found in Antarctica which came from Mars and bore traces of possible primitive life. To me it was obvious that it had been brought here by Martians (who live *under* the surface of Mars, of course)."

Carol spent several years working in a New York hospital before becoming a toy designer with a stuffed toy company and then a children's librarian. She has written several books for children, including *Saturday Night at the Dinosaur Stomp*. Carol lives in California with her husband and their two teenage sons.

SCOTT NASH points out that all the Martians in **Martian Rock** have very large noses. "They are very proud of their noses," he says. "So much so that the only clothes they wear are their 'schnoz' covers, which come in different colours and with different patterns."

Scott is involved in all aspects of media for children, being the co-founder of a design studio specializing in children's products, the creator of two animated TV series and a lecturer on children's culture and trends. His picture books include *Saturday Night at the Dinosaur Stomp*; *Oh, Tucker!* and two titles in the Brand New Readers series, *Monkey Business* and *Monkey Trouble*. He lives on an island in Maine, USA with his wife, Nancy.

Other Walker picture books

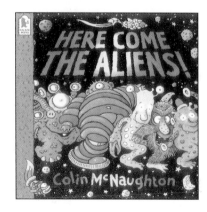

ISBN 0-7445-4394-0 (pb)

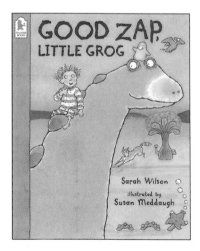

ISBN 0-7445-4068-2 (pb)

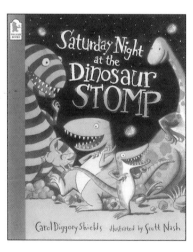

ISBN 0-7445-6345-3 (pb)

ISBN 0-7445-6362-3 (pb)